I0741338

This Nigger Is Crazy
Reginald "Dunbar" Walton

This Nigger IS Crazy

Reginald "Dunbar" Walton

This Nigger Is Crazy

Poems by: Reginald "Dunbar" Walton

Front Cover Picture by: Reginald "Dunbar" Walton

Design by: Jazzy Kitty Publishing

Logo Designs by: Andre M. Saunders/Leroy Grayson

Editor: Anelda L. Attaway

© 2012 Reginald Walton

ISBN 978-0-9851453-4-7

Library of Congress Control Number: 2012942567

For Worldwide Distribution. Printed in the United States of America. Published by Jazzy Kitty Greetings Marketing & Publishing, LLC. Utilizing Microsoft and Adobe Publishing Software. Utilizing Adobe and Microsoft Publishing Software.

Warning:

While writing this book, the author had to be rushed to the hospital to get his head checked.

DEDICATIONS

This book is dedicated to everyone that picks it up to read it because that's my soul purpose for writing. I appreciate your support.

TABLE OF CONTENTS

INTRODUCTION

In his second composition of fantastic and well versed poetry he goes into the psychotic mind of a mad man hell bent on seeking his own justice because of the burden that was put on his shoulders by this malice society in the United States. This is like God slapping you in the face with Truth: the truth being the reality of a man who society look down upon and thought was less of a man because he decided to follow his own light.

Experience the life and times of Dunbar as he takes you through these dark chambers of enlightenment. I would consider them dark chambers of enlightenment because in this collection of writings, the subjects of interest are usually very secretive and not something that you would want to discuss over Thanksgiving dinner.

So without farther a due, ladies and gentlemen I present to you…the one, the only, the hilarious…Mr. Reginald "Dunbar" Walton.

IN THE FACE PORTAL

Stressed the fuck out

And it's taking its toll

I need my black ass bitch

Like a wedding needs gold

I said be a mother to your child

Not realizing she needs a break

From being just that

When I was gone for a while

The times that she's stressed

I wish she would take it out on me

Release it how I did

When I was smashing her pussy

And stuck it in her butt

Fuck her hard - She couldn't walk

Collapsed in the floor crying

And couldn't strut

Fighting through sex
I gave her a serious pounding
Choked her throat with my dick
And my kids had her drowning

And the mental abuse that I provide
Is so dramatic
There's confusion and chaos
When we don't reach an understanding

But it's all for the better
Because I love my baby-cakes
So I let her meet Rihanna
A song she had to make

That's why I'm not settling
For an imitation copy
I be needing my mommy
And she be needing her poppy

I GOT STYLE

Brothers on death row

Waiting to be murdered

Screaming out there cells

Until the sentence served its purpose

Some study law

And try to overturn the judgment

That was given by a judge

That think he's more powerful than Jesus

Many take it as a joke

Until reality sets

You notice time getting shorter

And the police saying you next

It scares you to death

And some will search for a mystery

A spook in the sky

To come save them from enemies

While others stack up on merits
To try to balance their wrongs
Teach lessons to children
That will keep them from harm

I'm from the city of charm
And they're trying to revive the name
A change in the government
Or at least that's how it seem

That's how it seem
Because it was a change in the mind
Of leaders that lead
All the deaf, dumb and blind

It's amazing what can happen
When you study for a while
I learned the arts and crafts
I let you know I got style

THE INTERPRETER

I read the book of Daniel
Analyzing situations
Gabriel was prophesying
About the future of nations

Ruled by corrupt king
And those who went astray
Every day that we living
It's another judgment day

Revealed in a dream
Only the divine can interpret
So all the evil shit that men do
I hope that it's worth it

Daniel was like a Muslim
Praying three times a day
But the king was like God
He set in rules to obey

Nobody can pray to God

Or any other deity

You must go to the king

If you want any superiority

For the next 30 days

If you disobey you must pay

With your life

By sleeping in the lions dins and getting ate

Daniel was faithful

So he continued to pray

But because of his status

He had some people that hate

They told on him

Ratted on him like a jailhouse snitch

In the back of Daniel mind

I know he was saying: you BITCH!

RISING STAR

Now I'm returning from Mount Sinai
And I see the worship of calves
I'm feeling kind of pissed
So I break my tablets in half

As time past
I wonder how I got my situations
I risk my life for these people
My memory is now faded

Like Your God
Forgotten by the children of Israel
Whose real name is Jacob
You can check in the Bible

You'll find it in the same place
That God is a man
If you knowledge what I'm saying
It won't be hard to understand

Genesis Chapter 32, Verse 22

All the way to 32

Read it straight through

See, I speak the truth

And everything they won't teach

If God is not a man

Why the hell they praise Jesus

The government lied

They kept those slaves in the blind

We was never supposed to read

If we did, we must die

I'm hearing people saying

This a whole new millennium

They have a slave mentality

So they're living in the old one

WEST BASTARDS

West Baltimore's a trip
It's like they're living a movie
I got so many memories
I can be a little goofy

And often depressed
That's why I look to the future
Kids do what they do
Get in the way and they'll shoot you

An open market hustle
From the drug game to fruit
Driven by horses on carriages
To get that loot

It's a fucking war zone
But I call it my home
Walk to my destination
Then I'm never alone

Let's say you go to school
In a little place they call Sandtown
Half the class wouldn't make it
These brothers get gunned down

While the rest would get knocked
Trapped - caged by the beast
If you escape with intelligence
Ya considered rather unique

They love me in the hood
Even though I promised my brother
Now I spin most of my time
Apologizing to his mother

Who gives a fuck?
Every day in Armageddon is a war
It's like Lebron's first championship
We never get to score

NEW JUSTICE

The New Jerusalem's New Jersey
As I read in the Bible
The whole book of lamentations
Filled with nothing but sorrow

As it's said in the title
Vocabulary extensive
If you go against originals
Prices very expensive

Cost an arm and a leg
Plus so much stress in the head
Seek and you will find
Until the day that you're dead

Result of your parents' karma
You must find your way out of
Destructive situations
Like the war of Osama

You keep forgetting rules
That's why you keep getting punished
It's the little things in life
Like that meat in your stomach

Hear me now and listen later
I penetrate through my hater
You been warned about the swamp
But you wrestle with gators

Like the Bishop in Juice
Or the Fredro in Strapped
Sun, I take it back to Samson
That's how you get clapped

So keep that bullshit to yourself
Because it's not wanted here
Now is the time I build my nation
With some thoughts from my head

SOMETIMES I NEED TIME TO HEAL

One time, I popped my Shorty

'Cause she deserved it

I don't regret what I did

Because it really was worth it

Murdered in verses

I started fighting the government

So fuck what you think

I bring the drama to publics

But things start to change

Because the drama is real

My unspoken words

Produce potential to kill

So my feelings' involved

And now drama with my sister

Understand what I'm going through

Can deal with any nigga

Niggas never understand

So I keep it to myself

External type of torture

That can eliminate your health

Shit, I do what I do

But motherfuckers hate me for it

But my eyesight to the future

Like that chick Dion Warwick

I'll put you in my shoes

If you got a problem with it

Extraterrestrial intelligence

All that other shit irrelevant

While I'm popping my shit

Acting funny while getting money

Holding weight on my shoulders

It's not you, it's just me

LET DOWN, BUT I'VE LEARNED TO TRUST YOU

I'm trying to be your friend
But you really won't let me
I love you to death
But you're trying to forget me

Wishing we could start over
And do this whole thing right
With your mind, body, and soul
I'll be gentler at night

Wake up with you laying here
Right under my arms
I'd be the protection that you need
If ever a threat of harm

Don't let anybody do
Anything that I do to you
Because I'm your one and only sun
And you're reflecting my hues

I do the do when I bring the pain...

Have you insane

But regardless of situations

My love will be the same

You should've been my wife

The closest thing to me in life

But you shook and scared to death

And I ain't even that trife

I rather shine my light on you

And let you teach Nashuan some lessons

A step father to him

And we all get the blessings

I'm being patient with your love

But it's making me delirious

I'm sure you know my number

Baby, call me when you're serious

KNOWLEDGE VS. IGNORANCE

Niggas is fronting

Acting like they want problems

But they the first ones to switch

When their dumb ass hit bottom

Seen it a thousand times

I swear these bitches are the same

Take your kindness for weakness

Until you pop one in their brain

They living a lie

That's why they choose to get high

Escape from reality

Others use to get by

Whatever the case

You know that I can give a fuck

1970's style

Stick a dick in your butt

Take it how you want

When reality sets

Take a swim in the ocean

I guarantee I'll leave you wet

How I get this mentality

I've been through so many changes

Bringing drama too many

Attacking so many angles

I wish I was playing

But my life is not a joke

Systematically terminating

And eliminating hope

Feel the winds of the storm

So I'm constantly depressed

Catch this slug in the chest

I can eliminate your stress

TIME TRAVEL

I tried to be civilized

And deal with other guys

But it's hard for me to think

Because my brain cells are fried

Drama with sister

Because of distance between us

The future of this writer

Is really unheard of

I'm living original

And these motherfuckers are fraudulent

Whatever's whatever?

Just get my money for the rent

I do this for life

But motherfuckers don't understand that

It's more than a million different ways

To make a grip

Loose lips sink ships

Like them fake ass pimps

But rapping is cool

Just keep your gun by the hip

And I'm starting to settle down

As my nerves find order

I feel the shift in my consciousness

And my memory supporter

Taking off from here

Airplanes in atmospheres

Nobody can eliminate

The drama in my head

The head controls the body

As we enter time travel

A killah with the mind

To exit souls to a level

ATTEMPT TO COMFORT

Advertising that you want it

I'm telling you, you're not alone

And I see the picture clearly

You tickle my funny bones

Once again I'm locked in solitary

Being secluded from the masses

Divine-evils keep on fucking with me

I murder them bastards

I like what you saying

But some of it can get boring

After repetition speech

Going all night to the morning

You always seem to catch me

When I'm falling from grace

Like that black and white photo

On one knee in my face

Could your timing be worst?
Or maybe that's what I needed
'Cause when I sit back and think about it
It's like I got weeded

You my herbalize medicine
Slowly healing my mind
You got me drunk off ya love
A couple of bottles of wine

And you know I ain't playing
That's why I'm writing you now
Once again, I'm out my element
This ain't even my style

But if it put a smile on your face
I'm still down for the get down
Just pardon my actions
If I'm slow to understand

MY REPLY

Why slow to understand?

So many things on my mind

I guess that all comes a part of your life

When you doing time

One day I'll be free

But really, where the hell will you be?

Out of sight, out of mind

Or is it all for the money?

I got questions to ask

Because I questions myself

I'm unsure about my possibilities

In this life

Will this publisher publish me?

What I'ma do when I get out?

Will the public accept me?

How many do I have to knock out?

How much have they changed?
They don't talk to me no more
That was my goal from the start
It's just sometime I morn

Shall I go on...
With some of my personal feelings?
I was taught that you soft
If you show emotions in dealings

May be mis-education
From the those mis-educated
Shit, coming from my hood
It's a survival translation

So it's developed in my being
But I'm always willing to change
In the evolution of man
To survive won't be the same

TEN MINUTES LATER

What's up Devil?
They sent me to E.C.I. prematurely
Now they kicking my black ass out
With authority

I thought the judge was sending you
To a drug program
What happened to that situation?
You had a decent hand

That pen pal service - How can I say?
Bullshit!
You warned me of a scam
I had nothing to lose - I tried it

But they never came through
And caught a death wish or two
Now I'm sitting on administrative
Writing to you

Speaking of which
What's up with your devilettes?
The one fresh out of prison
Hot like red corvettes

And that other young lady
With an origin of Russia
You told her to put me on
I wasn't in her discussion

I stick to myself
I don't be hollering out the door
Me and this system about even
But we'll see the final score

Allah See Equality
I elevate my mentality
What's the world through your eyes?
Put me D with your reality

BITTEN AP

Justice Allah Why
The way the public seem to cry
You heard Ready 2 Die
Suicidal thoughts 41st side

What goes through your mind?
On a day to day basis
As you open your eyes
In fanatical faces

I be learning so much
And adding on when I can
What I thought was illusion
Is about as real as the wind

Therefore it's reality
I accept it as such
Embracing everything
Even that which I can't touch

But your focus is money
I give a fuck about riches
In this material world
My pockets could be a little thicker

That's a personal situation
Like a woman's menstruation
These times comes and go
Come and go purification

I study cycles of life
The evolution of man
As an individual
I keep on growing like a hand

Look at the tips
Elevation on the black side
Infinite eye
Collaborating U-N-I

SYSTEMATIC

Fuck ya anticipation

My mind trapped in meditation

Elevating my mind

'Cause between me and you...

A separation

You stuck on stupid

I come through with arrows

Just like I'm cupid

Pierce your heart with no love

And you're physical

I'm now through with

Penetrating your skull

Like the Gray's illuminating intelligence

Engulf your soul with flame

Forever burning kind of hellish

Are you retarded or what?

Are you illiterate dip shit?

Do you like feeling pain?

I'll be the first to give quick

Plus ya hot ass sister

I got plans to get with her

I'll murder the bitch

If she don't make me get richer

You crossed paths with the wrong

You should've stayed in your lane

Now a genocidal maniac

Gunning for you and your dame

And you know it's a shame

When guns hitting your resident

With intension to kill

Spill blood and its evident

I ain't playing no games

Mind state is terminator

That's what you get when you choose on me...

Eliminated

TALKING BACK

So what's up with you?

I been thinking 'bout your white ass

With your sexual energy

I'll give you the dick of Shabazz

And whoever don't like it

I guess they can kiss my ass

And suck my dick while they at it

After I pull it from your crack

Nasty

Nasty as I want to be

I'll punish the pussy

And then I'll come and punish pussy

You got some beautiful lips

A nice ass

A couple tits

A helluva attitude

That combines to swell my dick

Rampant and savage

My character is animalistic

That's what you do to me bitch

Doggy style while I'm dicking

But when I come to my senses

And the ball sack is drained

And we have a conversation

Would you still feel the same?

I'm divine

So the lust can only last for so long

The King of Queens will be the thing

Until the dirt and we gone

Plus I want to fuck Julie

And keep her under my wing

A one night stand with the rest

I'm dead serious

No bullshit

JOB

Job was one of 85

And it shows in his written wisdom

The Gods tried to teach him

With a precise precision

Although he was faithful

He still believed in a mystery

So when things started happening

He had no understanding

Satan was tempting

And granted control of possessions

So when god let him hurt him

He asked him, what the fuck happen

When the Lord gave him answers

He didn't believe it himself

Well, what the fuck was he praying for?

If he didn't want help

Satan penetrated deep

And he had him suicidal

He made a bet with the God

For the soul of Job the Prophet

Manifested as friends

They tried to make him comprehend

But dude was blind, deaf, and dumb

The light was right in front of him

2 Divine Beings

Made a deal for his soul

Look at what you wager

You don't find it valuable

The whole thing was a test

Just like our everyday life

This wisdom is sharp

You probably think it's a knife

WHY YOU DO THAT?!?

I know your story

And how you're all alone in this world

You never knew your biologicals

And got played by them girls

You were raised by a family

But they was lying the whole time

You thought you came from a pussy

The woman said it ain't mine

You officially an alien

Then you learn a discovery

Extraterrestrial experiments

Playing the public like dummies

But you feel just as duped

Because your life was a lie

Now revenge in your eye

These bastards must die

So you pick up a weapon
And man you do what you gotta
Attempted to murder motherfuckers
You can call it kamikaze

Eye for an eye
Like Moses in the Bible
All that blood on your hands
And your actions are suicidal

Honorable title
And your public can't face the truth
They gave you false memories
So you disconnect their root

Throwing chi
Like Chung Li
Fighting in the street
Your whole style is methodic
And you can rhyme it to the beat

COPY CAT

Now can you just imagine having...
A father like this
That would never make a move
Unless you first did the shit

Like if you get a group of girls
He would get a group of girls
He would mimic your actions
And even copy all your words

So there's no one to guide you
Because he want to be you
You living a backwards cipher
So who's parenting who

The only benefit from him
Is going to work and paying bills
But the stress is building up
To the point you want to kill

Plus he says you not his son
As a constant reminder
He'll punch you in your dome
Just as soon as he find ya

Fucking a broad
Yeah, it's forbidden as a youth
They rather see me homosexual
So they can laugh with the proof

So your father not a father
Until the day you're in the casket
You make your way through this world
With the public calling you a bastard

And the shit never rest
Because they keep doing the same
Plus they look at you strange
So you don't have a fucking friend

TOUCH ME, TEASE ME, SUCK ME, PLEASE ME

To the black ass bitch

I used to lust in the past

I would shine on the moon

And make the earth feel the wrath

Thinking about ya nasty ass

Sucking my dick

When you juggling nuts

Have you learned to swallow or do you spit

Its been a few years

I know somebody tapped your anal

You can't be that nice

To be so sexy saying 'no'

Shit, it's all experimental

They had me locked up with criminals

With no one to love me

So I can be sentimental

At least certain times

Because I harden my heart

Then I realized

Your stupid ass still love me in the dark

How do I know?

I'll keep my sources to myself

I started to understand your style

So you can play with your bottom shelf

You had a living space for me

I wonder is it still open

Picture me and you just chilling

No joking

I got so many angles

To execute what I'm saying

This is just one of them

Now bitch stop playing

EVERYBODY'S AN ACTOR

In the middle of this discussion

I'ma stop for a while

To really give it some thought

On why I'm attracted to your smile

We'll cover the basis

Sexy

Hypnotizing you might be

I look at your thighs

And glance through time where I might be

You got some good pussy

Starting slow to slide up on me

But the inside of your thighs

Is shining with the stuff that's slimy

That's the shit that I like

But what will happen when it's over

Get addicted to the feeling

But we both have to sober

It's your eyesight that captured me

It makes me want to explode

The inner rhythms of your mind

Make me want to learn more

But what the hell for

What attracts a man to a woman?

I mean...

What makes us love?

Get together and have children

I got a deep mind

That goes from here to my brother

That lives by a star

Light years away by another

But when it's exposed

Tell me how would you feel?

It's the core of the person

I'm afraid you won't like for real

THINK ABOUT IT

What's up chocolate titties?

This is Mr. Goodbar

I got a different persona

I changed my name to Dunbar

Elevating my dome

I try to murder propaganda

On genocidal missions

85's: they like to slander

Talking about nothing

All their conversations domestic

I'm a scientist baby

So my elements can make it hectic

But since this light to the earth

I put my dick in the crater

And shoot for the seed

Rise like cream a little later

Gerber got a plan

You can invest in the future

Use the grow-up plan

So Shorty won't become a loser

And try to be healthier

Avoid the medical problems

Most only think about now

So they don't even bother

Look at your father

Equipped with heartaches and strokes

Act like a savage

Look at the murder I wrote

It's funny how ya'll left me

When I needed ya'll help

It happened for a reason

I'm doing well for myself

RISEN AWAKE

Look Shorty, here's the scoop
Yeah I'm here to keep it real
I'm about as real as it get
Because I make them suckers peel

Today you will be judged
By the true and living God
That's why I traveled the universe
Collecting Knowledge from the Stars

If you an 85
Then you don't want to hear it
Just like the children of Israel
Until I damage your spirit

I'll beat you down with the heat
Then send some light through the dark
You see, it always takes massacres
For people to trust in the God

But Allah is forgiving
Also known as the merciful
But you so disobedient
Please don't make me have to hurt ya

Don't take it as a threat
It's prophesied that I return
Decisive battles in the sky
I'm here to make your soul burn

From Abraham to Moses
2000 years on this earth
The same length of time
Moses, Jesus, My Birth

You probably think it's a game
Be stupid and go against me
The most gracious, most merciful
And I want you riding with me

VENOM THOUGHT FROM THE ESSENCE

It's like I don't know why

I waste my time in these places

My wisdom enter one ear

And out the other side of your faces

So what's the basis?

When my intentions are for the righteous

Fighting political propaganda

The public call exciting

It's the 14th of October

And my mental is sober

Yet high off reality

Drinking venom like a cobra

I thought I told ya

Everything you see was manifested

From a single from of thought

And we call it the essence

That's where ya heading

So while ya here just learn ya lessons

Because the mind and soul exist

When the physical's shedded

That's a hard lesson

And many can't even deal with the fact

Transcending is inevitable

You know I'm right and exact

That's why when niggaz get shot

Their hard wayz go out the window

Instantaneous change

It's religiously a miracle

You see

Everything that happens on this earth is for a reason

I rather conquer myself

Than satisfy the hunting season

COMPLICATED DECISIONS

As the stimuli sets in

I realize I'm not shit

In a world full of mischief

I'm telling God to suck my dick

It's totally wrong

But I proceed with the murders

Hittin' niggas with shit

They ain't never seen or heard of

Like a mystery God

I work in mysterious ways

My entourage is angels

And they always get their pay

Beefing with the public

So many go against me

Friends are now enemies

Little

To no family

So I attack like the sun
You take your walk through the sand
Sparking 93,000,000 miles
Across the hottest land

The way that I shine
Only the strong will survive
That's why I'm writing this rhyme
So I won't be losing my mind

Its nights like this
I'm bound to catch 100 years
A total disregard for life
I feel no comfort from peers

So now I'll roam the streets
Until I do for myself
Or maybe I'd bite the bullet
I might off my fucking self

ABOUT THE AUTHOR

Reginald Walton was born in Portsmith, Virginia and immediately moved to Baltimore, Maryland where he grew up at. He spent his childhood traveling up and down the East Coast and never stayed in one neighborhood for more than one year at a time.

By the age of 9, he gravitated toward a life of crime. At the age of 15, he was charged as an adult for an attempt to murder; there he was - a child incarcerated with a bunch of grown men that society considered the worst of the worst, but they saw the potential in him and began to teach him. He would listen attentively and decided to make a change. The rest is in his writings. I hope you enjoy.